Balloons Go Pop!

Story by Beverley Randell
Illustrations by Liz Alger

"The green balloon is for me," said Nick.

"The blue balloon is for me," said Kate.

"And here is a red balloon

for me," said James.

"Look at my balloon,"

shouted Nick.

"My balloon is up in a tree."

Pop!

"Oh, no!" said Nick.

"My balloon

is up in a tree, too,"

shouted Kate.

Pop!

"Oh, no!" said Kate.

James said,

"**My** balloon

is not going to pop."

"Here is my red balloon!"